Anthony is a popular and prolific children's writer whose books now sell in more than a dozen countries around the world. He has won numerous prizes for his books, which include *Stormbreaker* (shortlisted for the 2000 Children's Book Award) and its sequels *Point Blanc*, *Skeleton Key*, *Eagle Strike* and *Scorpia* about reluctant teenage MI6 spy Alex Rider; *Groosham Grange* and its sequel *Return to Groosham Grange*; *Granny* (shortlisted for the 1994 Children's Book Award); and the Diamond Brothers trilogy – *The Falcon's Malteser* (which has been filmed with the title *Just Ask for Diamond*), followed by *South by South East* (which was dramatized in six parts on TV) and *Public Enemy Number Two* – to which *I Know What You Did Last Wednesday* and two other short novels, *The French Confection* and *The Blurred Man*, have been added.

Anthony also writes extensively for TV, with credits including the hit series *Murder in Mind*, as well as *Foyle's War*, *Midsomer Murders*, *Poirot* and *Murder Most Horrid*, and he has been described by the *Radio Times* as "a one man crime-wave". He is married to the television producer Jill Green and lives in north London with his two children, Nicholas and Cassian, and their dog, Unlucky.

Other Diamond Brothers books
The Falcon's Malteser
South by South East
Public Enemy Number Two
The Blurred Man
The French Confection

The Alex Rider books
Stormbreaker
Point Blanc
Skeleton Key
Eagle Strike
Scorpia

Other books by the same author
The Devil and His Boy
Granny
Groosham Grange
Return to Groosham Grange
The Switch

I Know What You Did Last Wednesday

ANTHONY HOROWITZ

WALKER BOOKS
AND SUBSIDIARIES
LONDON · BOSTON · SYDNEY · AUCKLAND

First published 2002 by Walker Books Ltd
87 Vauxhall Walk, London SE11 5HJ

This edition published 2003

4 6 8 10 9 7 5

This book has been typeset in Sabon

Printed in Great Britain by Cox & Wyman Ltd, Reading, Berkshire

British Library Cataloguing in Publication Data:
a catalogue record for this book is
available from the British Library

ISBN 0-7445-9038-8

www.walkerbooks.co.uk

CONTENTS

AN INVITATION

I like horror stories – but not when they happen to me. If you've read my other adventures, you'll know that I've been smothered in concrete, thrown in jail with a dangerous lunatic, tied to a railway line, almost blown up, chased through a cornfield dodging machine-gun bullets, poisoned in Paris ... and all this before my fourteenth birthday. It's not fair. I do my homework. I clean my teeth twice a day. Why does everyone want to kill me?

But the worst thing that ever happened to me began on a hot morning in July. It was the first week of the summer holidays and there I was, as usual, stuck with my big brother Tim, the world's most unsuccessful private detective. Tim had just spent a month helping with security at the American Embassy in Grosvenor Square and even now I'm not sure how he'd decided that there was a bomb in the ambassador's car. Anyway, just as the ambassador was about to get in, Tim had grabbed hold of him and hurled him out of the way – which would have been heroic if there had been a bomb (there wasn't) and if Tim hadn't managed to throw the unfortunate man in front of a passing bus. The ambassador was now in hospital. And Tim was out of work.

So there we were at the breakfast table with Tim reading the morning post while I counted out the cornflakes. We were down to our last packet and it had to last us another week. That allowed us seventeen flakes each but as a treat I'd allowed Tim to keep the free toy. There was a handful of letters that morning and so far they'd all been bills.

"There's a letter from Mum," Tim said.

"Any money?"

"No..."

He quickly read the letter. It was strange to think that my mum and dad were still in Australia and that I would have been with them if I hadn't slipped off the plane and gone to stay with Tim. My dad was a door-to-door salesman, selling doors. He had a house in Sydney with three bedrooms and forty-seven doors. It had been two years now since I had seen him.

"Mum says you're welcome to visit," Tim said. "She says the door is always open."

"Which one?" I asked.

He picked up the last letter. I could see at

once that this wasn't a bill. It came in a square, white envelope made out of the sort of paper that only comes from the most expensive trees. The address was handwritten: a fountain-pen, not a biro. Tim weighed it in his hand. "I wonder what this is," he said.

"It's an envelope, Tim," I replied. "It's what letters come in."

"I mean ... I wonder who it's from!" He smiled. "Maybe it's a thank-you letter from the American ambassador."

"Why should he thank you? You threw him under a bus!"

"Yes, but I sent him a bunch of grapes in hospital."

"Just open it, Tim," I said.

Tim grabbed hold of a knife, and – with a dramatic gesture – sliced open the mysterious envelope.

After we'd finished bandaging his left leg, we examined the contents. First, there was an invitation, printed in red ink on thick white card.

Dear Herbert, it began. Tim Diamond was, of course, only the name he called himself. His real name was Herbert Simple.

It has been many years since we met, but I would like to invite you to a reunion of old boys and girls from St Egbert's Comprehensive, which will take place from Wednesday 9th to Friday 11th July. I am sure you are busy but I am so keen to see you again that I will pay you £1,000 to make the journey to Scotland. I also enclose a ticket for the train.

Your old friend,
Rory McDougal

Crocodile Island, Scotland

Tim tilted the envelope. Sure enough, a first-class train ticket slid out onto the table.

"That's fantastic!" Tim exclaimed. "A first-class ticket to Scotland." He examined the ticket. "And back again! That's even better!"

"Wait a minute," I said. "Who is Rory McDougal?" But even as I spoke, I thought the name was familiar.

"We were at school together, in the same class. Rory was brilliant. He came first in maths. He was so clever, he passed all his exams without even reading the questions. After he left school, he invented the pocket calculator – which was just as well, because he made so much money he needed a pocket calculator to count it."

"McDougal Industries." Now I knew where I'd heard the name. McDougal had been in the newspapers. The man was a multi-Mcmillionaire.

"When did you last see him?" I asked.

"It must have been on prize-giving day, about ten years ago," Tim said. "He went to university, I joined the police."

Tim had only spent a year with the police but in that time the crime rate had doubled. He didn't often talk about it but I knew that he had once put together an identikit picture that had led to the arrest of the Archbishop of Canterbury. He'd been transferred to the mounted police but that had only lasted a few weeks before his horse resigned. Then he'd become a private detective – and of course, *he* had hardly made millions. If you added up all the money Tim had ever made and put it in a bank, the bank wouldn't even notice.

"Are you going?" I asked.

Tim flicked a cornflake towards his mouth. It disappeared over his shoulder. "Of course I'm going," he said. "Maybe McNoodle will offer me a job. Head of Security on Alligator Island."

"Crocodile Island, Tim." I picked up the invitation. "What about me?"

"Sorry, kid. I didn't see your name on the envelope."

"Maybe it's under the stamp." Tim said nothing, so I went on, "You can't leave me here."

"Why not?"

"I'm only fourteen. It's against the law."

Tim frowned. "I won't tell if you won't tell."

"I will tell."

"Forget it, Nick. McStrudel is my old schoolfriend. He went to my old school. It's my name on the envelope and you can argue all you like. But this time, I'm going alone."

We left King's Cross station on the morning of the 9th.

Tim sat next to the window, looking sulky. I was sitting opposite him. I had finally persuaded him to swap the first-class ticket for two second-class ones, which at least allowed me to travel free. You may think it strange that I should have wanted to join Tim on a journey heading several hundred miles north. But there was something about the invitation that bothered me. Maybe it was the letter, written in ink the colour of blood. Maybe it was the name – Crocodile Island. And then there was the money. The invitation might have sounded innocent enough, but why was McDougal paying Tim £1,000 to get on the train? I had a feeling that there might be more to this than a school reunion. And for that matter, why would anyone in their right mind want to be reunited with Tim?

I was also curious. It's not every day that you get to meet a man like Rory McDougal. Computers, camcorders, mobile phones and DVD players ... they all came stamped with the initials RM. And every machine that sold made McDougal a little richer.

Apparently the man was something of a recluse. A few years back he'd bought himself an island off the Scottish coast, somewhere to be alone. There had been pictures of it in all the newspapers. The island was long and narrow with two arms jutting out and a twisting tail. Apparently, that was how it had got its name.

Tim didn't say much on the journey. To cheer him up, I'd bought him a *Beano* comic and perhaps he was having trouble with the long words. It took us about four hours to get to Scotland and it took another hour before I noticed. There were no signs, no frontier post, no man in a kilt playing the bagpipes and munching haggis as the train went past. It was only when the ticket collector asked us for our tickets and Tim couldn't understand a word he was saying that I knew we must be close. Sure enough, a few minutes later the train slowed down and Tim got out. Personally, I would have waited until the train had actually stopped, but I suppose he was over-excited.

Fortunately he was only bruised and we managed the short walk down to the harbour where an old fishing boat was waiting for us. The boat was called the *Silver Medal* and a small crowd of people were waiting to go on board.

"My God!" one of them exclaimed. "It's Herbert Simple! I never thought I'd see *him* again!"

The man who had spoken was fat and bald, dressed in a three-piece suit. If he ate much more, it would soon be a four-piece suit. His trousers were already showing the strain. His name, it turned out, was Eric Draper. He was a lawyer.

Tim smiled. "I changed my name," he announced. "It's Tim Diamond now."

They all had a good laugh at that.

"And who is he?" Eric asked. I suddenly realized he was looking at me.

"That's my kid brother, Nick."

"So what are you doing now … Tim?" one of the women asked in a high-pitched voice. She had glasses and long, curly hair and such large teeth that she seemed to have trouble closing her mouth. Her name was Janet Rhodes.

Tim put on his "don't mess with me" face. Unfortunately, it just made him look seasick. "Actually," he drawled, "I'm a private detective."

"Really?" Eric roared with laughter. His suit shuddered and one of the buttons flew off. "I can't believe Rory invited you here too. As I recall, you were the stupidest boy at St Egbert's. I still remember your performance as Hamlet in the school play."

"What was so stupid about that?" I asked.

"Nothing. Except everyone else was doing Macbeth."

One of the other women stepped forward.

She was small and drab-looking, dressed in a mousy coat that had seen better days. She was eating a chocolate flake. "Hello … Tim!" she said shyly. "I bet you don't remember me!"

"Of course I remember you!" Tim exclaimed. "You're Lisa Beach!"

"No I'm not! I'm Sylvie Binns." She looked disappointed. "You gave me my first kiss behind the bike shed. Don't you remember?"

Tim frowned. "I remember the bike shed…" he said.

There was a loud blast from the boat and the captain appeared, looking over the side. He had one leg, one eye and a huge beard. All that was missing was the parrot and he could have got a job in any pantomime in town. "All aboard!" he shouted. "Departing for Crocodile Island!"

We made our way up the gangplank. The boat was old and smelly. So was the captain. The eight of us stood on the deck while he pulled up the anchor, and a few minutes later we were off, the engine rattling as if it was about to fall out of the boat. It occurred to me that the *Silver Medal* was a strange choice of boat for a multi-millionaire. What had happened to the deluxe yacht? But nobody else had noticed, so I said nothing.

Apart from Eric, Janet and Sylvie, there were three other people on board: two more women and another man, a fit-looking black guy dressed in jeans and a sweatshirt.

"That's Mark Tyler," Tim told me as we cut through the waves, leaving the mainland behind us. "He came first at sport at St Egbert's..."

I knew the name. Tyler had been in the British Olympic athletics team at Atlanta.

"He used to run to school and run home again," Tim went on. "He was so fast, he used to overtake the school bus. When he went cross-country running, he actually left the country, which certainly made the headmaster very cross. He's a brilliant sportsman!"

That just left the two other women.

Brenda Blake was an opera singer and looked it. Big and muscular, she had the sort of arms you'd expect to find on a Japanese wrestler – or perhaps around his belly.

Libby Goldman was big and blonde and worked in children's TV, presenting a television programme called *Libby's Lounge*. She sang, danced, juggled and did magic tricks ... and all this before we'd even left the quay. It was a shame that in real life we couldn't turn her off.

The journey took about an hour, by which time the coast of Scotland had become just a grey smudge behind us. Slowly Crocodile Island sneaked up on us. It was about half a mile long, rising to a point at what must have been its "tail", with sheer cliffs sweeping down into the sea. There were six jagged pillars of rock at this end, making a landing impossible. But at the other end, in the shelter of the crocodile's arm, someone had built a jetty. As the boat drew in, I noticed a security camera watching us from above.

"Here we are, ladies and gentlemen," the captain announced from somewhere behind his beard. "I wish you all a very pleasant stay on Crocodile Island. I do indeed! I'll be coming back for you in a couple of days. My name is Captain Randle, by the way. Horatio Randle. It's been a pleasure having you lovely people on my boat. You remember me, now!"

"Aren't you coming with us?" Eric demanded.

"No, sir. I'm not invited," Captain Randle replied. "I live on the mainland. But I'll be back to collect you in a couple of days. I'll see you then!"

We disembarked. The boat pulled out and headed back the way it had come. The eight of us were left on the island, wondering what was going to happen next.

"So where's old Rory?" Brenda asked.

"Maybe we should walk up to the house," Sylvie suggested. She was the only one of them who didn't have a full-time job. She had told Tim that she was a housewife, and was carrying three photographs of her husband and three more of her house.

16

"Bit of a cheek," Eric muttered. From the look of him, walking wasn't something he did often.

"Best foot forward!" Janet said cheerily. Apparently she worked as a hairdresser, and her own hair was dancing in the wind. As indeed was Libby.

We walked. Sylvie might have called it a house but I would have said it was a castle that Rory had bought for himself on his island retreat. It was built out of grey brick: a grand, sprawling building with towers and battlements and even gargoyles gazing wickedly out of the corners. We reached the front door. It was solid oak, as thick as a tree and half as welcoming.

"I wonder if we should knock?" Tim asked.

"To hell with that!" Eric pushed and the door swung open.

We found ourselves in a great hall with a black and white floor, animal heads on the walls and a roaring fire in the hearth. A grandfather clock chimed four times. I looked at my watch – it was actually ten past three. I was already beginning to feel uneasy. Apart from the crackle of the logs and the ticking of the clock, the house was silent. It felt empty. No Rory, no Mrs Rory, no butler, no cook. Just us.

"Hello?" Libby called out. "Is there anyone at home?"

"It-doesn't-look-as-if-there's-anyone-here,"

Mark said. At least, I think that's what he said. Speaking was something else that he did very fast. Whole sentences came out of his mouth as a single word.

"This is ridiculous," Eric snapped. "I suggest we split up and try and find Rory. Maybe he's asleep upstairs."

So we all went our separate ways. Mark and Eric headed off through different doors. Libby Goldman went into the kitchen. Tim and I went upstairs. It was only now that we were inside it that I realized just how big this house was. It had five staircases, doors everywhere and so many corridors that we could have been walking through a maze. And if it looked like a castle from the outside, inside it was like a museum. There was more furniture than you'd find in a department store. Antique chairs and sofas stood next to cupboards and sideboards and tables of every shape and size. There were so many oil paintings that you could hardly see the walls. Rory also seemed to have a fondness for ancient weapons – I had only been in the place a few minutes but already I had seen crossbows and muskets and flintlock pistols mounted on wooden plaques. On the first floor there was a stuffed bear holding an Elizabethan gun ... a blunderbuss. The stairs and upper landing were covered in thick, red carpet which muffled every sound. In the distance I could hear Janet calling out Rory's

18

name but it was difficult to say if she was near or far away. Suddenly we were lost and very much on our own.

We reached a corner where there was a suit of dull silver armour standing guard; a knight with a shield but no sword.

"I don't like it," I said.

"I think it's a very nice suit of armour," Tim replied.

"I'm not talking about the armour, Tim," I said. "I'm talking about the whole island. Why isn't there anyone here to meet us? And why did your friend send that old fishing boat to pick us up?"

Tim smiled. "Relax, kid," he said. "The house is a bit quiet, that's all. But my sixth sense would tell me if there was something wrong, and right now I'm feeling fine..."

Just then there was a high-pitched scream from another part of the second floor. It was Brenda. She screamed and screamed again.

"How lovely!" Tim exclaimed. "Brenda's singing for us! I think that's Mozart, isn't it?"

"It's not Mozart, Tim," I shouted, beginning to run towards the sound. "She's screaming for help! Come on!"

We ran down the corridor and round the corner. That was when we saw Brenda, standing in front of an open bedroom door. She had stopped screaming now but her face was white

19

and her hands were tearing at her hair. At the same time, Libby and Sylvie appeared, coming up the stairs. And Eric was also there, pushing his way forward to see what the fuss was about.

Tim and I reached the doorway. I looked inside.

The room had a red carpet. It took me a couple of seconds to realize that the room had once had a yellow carpet. It was covered in blood. There was more blood on the walls and on the bed. There was even blood on the blood.

And there was McDougal. I'm afraid it was the end of the story for Rory. The sword that had killed him was lying next to him and I guess it must have been taken from the suit of armour.

Brenda screamed again and pulled out a handful of her own hair.

Eric stood back, gasping.

Libby burst into tears.

And Tim, of course, fainted.

There were just the eight of us, trapped on Crocodile Island. And I had to admit, our reunion hadn't got off to a very good start.

AFTER DARK

"It was horrible," Tim groaned. "It was horrible. Rory McPoodle ... he was in pieces!"

"I don't want to hear about it, Tim," I said. Actually, it was too late. He'd already told me twenty times.

"Why would anyone *do* that?" he demanded. "What sort of person would do that?"

"I'm not sure," I muttered. "How about a dangerous lunatic?"

Tim nodded. "You could be right," he said.

We were sitting in our bedroom. We knew it was the bedroom that McDougal had prepared for us because it had Tim's name on the door. There were seven bedrooms on the same floor, each one of them labelled for the arriving guests. This room was square, with a high ceiling and a window with a low balcony looking out over a sea that was already grey and choppy as the sun set and the evening drew in.

There was a four-poster bed, a heavy tapestry and the sort of wallpaper that could give you bad dreams. There was also something else I'd noticed and it worried me.

"Look at this, Tim," I said. I pointed at the bedside table. "There's a telephone socket here – but no telephone. What does that tell you?"

"The last person who slept in this room stole the telephone?"

"Not exactly. I think the telephone has been taken to stop us making any calls."

"Why would anyone do that?"

"To stop us reporting the death of Rory McDougal to the police."

Tim considered. "You mean … someone knew we were coming…" he began.

"Exactly. And they also knew we'd be stuck here. At least until the boat came back."

It was a nasty thought. I was beginning to have lots of nasty thoughts, and the worst one was this: someone had killed Rory McDougal, but had it happened before we arrived on the island? Or had he been killed by one of the people from the boat? As soon as we had arrived at the house, we had all split up. For at least ten minutes nobody had known where anybody else was, which meant that any one of us could have found Rory and killed him before the others arrived.

Along with Tim and myself, there were now six people on the island … six and several halves if you counted Rory. Eric Draper, Janet Rhodes, Sylvie Binns, Mark Tyler, Brenda Blake and Libby Goldman. Tim hadn't seen any of them in ten years and knew hardly anything about them. Could one of them be a crazed killer? Could one of them have planned this whole thing?

I looked at my watch. It was ten to seven. We left the room and went back downstairs.

Eric Draper had called a meeting in the dining-room at seven o'clock. I don't know who had put him in charge but I guessed he had decided himself.

"He was head boy at school," Tim told me. "He was always telling everyone what to do. Even the teachers used to do what he said."

"What was Rory McDougal like as a boy?"

"Well ... he was young."

"That's very helpful, Tim. I mean ... was he popular?"

"Yes. Except he once had a big row with Libby Goldman. He tried to kiss her in biology class and she attacked him with a bicycle pump."

"But she wouldn't kill him just because of that, would she?"

"You should have seen where she put the bicycle pump!"

In fact Libby was alone in the dining-room when we arrived for the meeting. She was sitting in a chair at the end of a black, polished table that ran almost the full length of the room. Portraits of bearded men in different shades of tartan looked down from the walls. A chandelier hung from the ceiling.

She looked up as we came in. Her eyes were red. Either she had been crying or she had bad hay fever – and I hadn't noticed any hay on Crocodile Island. She was smoking a cigarette – or trying to. Her hands were shaking so much she had trouble getting it into her mouth.

"What are we going to do?" she wailed. "It's so horrible! I knew I shouldn't have accepted Rory's invitation!"

"Why did you?" I asked. "If you didn't like him..."

"Well ... he's interesting. He's rich. I thought he might appear on my television programme – *Libby's Lounge*."

"I watch that!" Tim exclaimed.

"But it's a children's programme," Libby said.

Tim blushed. "Well ... I mean ... I've seen it. A bit of it."

"I've never heard of it," I muttered.

Libby's eyes went redder.

Then three of the others came in: Janet Rhodes, Mark Tyler and Brenda Blake.

"I've been trying to call the mainland on my mobile phone," Janet announced. "But I can't get a signal."

"I can't get a signal either," agreed Mark,

speaking as quickly as ever. He sort of shimmered in front of me and suddenly he was sitting down.

"There is no signal on this island."

"And no phone in my room," Janet said.

"No phone in any room!" The singer was looking pale and scared. Of course, she was the one who had found the body. Looking at her, I saw that it would be a few months before she sang in a concert hall. She probably wouldn't have the strength to sing in the bath.

Somewhere a clock struck seven and Eric Draper waddled into the room. "Are we all here?" he asked.

"I'm here!" Tim called out, as helpful as ever.

"I think there's one missing," I said.

Eric Draper did a quick head count. At least everyone in the room still had their heads. "Sylvie isn't here yet," he said. He scowled. You could tell he was the sort of man who expected everyone to do exactly what he said. "We'll have to wait for her."

"She was always late for everything," Janet muttered. She had slumped into a chair next to Libby. "I don't know how she managed to come first in chemistry. She was always late for class."

"I saw her in her room a few moments ago," Mark said. "She was sitting on the bed. She looked upset."

"I'm upset!" Eric said. "We're all upset!

25

Well, let's begin without her." He cleared his throat as if we were the jury and he was about to begin his summing up. "We are clearly in a very awkward situation here. We've been invited to this island, only to discover that our host, Rory McDougal, has been murdered. We can't call the police because it would seem that there are no telephones and none of our mobiles can get a signal. Unless we can find a boat to get back to the mainland, we're stuck here until Captain Randle – or whatever his name was – arrives to pick us up. The only good news is that there's plenty of food in the house. I've looked in the kitchen. This is a comfortable house. We should be fine here."

"Unless the killer strikes again," I said.

Everyone looked at me. "What makes you think he'll do that?" Eric demanded.

"It's a possibility," I said. "And anyway, 'he' could be a 'she'."

I noticed Libby shivered when I said that – but to be frank she'd been shivering a lot recently.

"Did Rory invite you here too?" Mark asked.

"Not exactly. He invited Tim, and Tim couldn't leave me on my own at home. So I came along for the ride."

Eric scowled for a second time. Scowling suited him. "I wouldn't have said this place was suitable for children," he said.

"Murder isn't suitable for children," I agreed. "But I'm stuck here with you and it seems to me that we've all been set up. No phones! That has to be on purpose. All the rooms were prepared for us, with our names on the doors. And now, like you say, we're stuck here. Suppose the killer is here too?"

"That's not possible," Brenda whispered. But she didn't sound like she believed herself.

"Maybe Rory wasn't murdered," Tim suggested. "Maybe it was an accident."

"You mean someone accidentally chopped him to pieces?" I asked.

Janet glanced at the door. She was looking nervous. A hairdresser having a bad hair day. "Perhaps we should go and find Sylvie," she suggested.

Nobody said anything. Then, as one, we hurried out of the room.

We went back upstairs. Sylvie's room was halfway down the corridor, two doors away from our own. It was closed. Tim knocked. There was no reply. "She could have fallen asleep," he said.

"Just open the door, Tim," I suggested.

He opened it. Sylvie's room was a similar size to ours but with more modern furniture, an abstract painting on the wall and two single beds. Her case was standing beside the wall, unopened. As my eyes travelled towards her, I noticed a twist of something silver lying in the middle of the yellow carpet. But I didn't have time to mention it.

Sylvie was lying on her back, one hand flung out. When I had first seen her I had thought her small and silent. Now she was smaller and dreadfully still. I felt Mark push past me, entering the room.

"Is she...?" he began.

"Yes," Tim said. "She's asleep."

"I don't think so, Tim," I said.

Eric went over to her and took her wrist between a podgy finger and thumb. "She has no pulse," he said. He leant over her. "She's not breathing."

Tim's mouth fell open. "Do you think she's ill?" he asked.

"She's dead, Tim," I said. Two murders in one day. And it wasn't even Tim's bedtime.

Libby burst into tears. It was getting to be a habit with her. At least Brenda didn't scream again. At this close range, I'm not sure my eardrums could have taken it.

"What are we going to do?" someone asked. I wasn't sure who it was and it didn't matter anyway. Because right then I didn't have any idea.

"It might have been a heart attack," Tim said. "Maybe the shock of what happened to Rory..."

Darkness had fallen on Crocodile Island. It

had slithered across the surface of the sea and thrown itself over the house. Now and then a full moon came out from behind the clouds and for a moment the waves would ripple silver before disappearing into inky blackness. Tim and I were sitting on our four-poster bed. It looked like we were going to have to share it. Two posters each.

Maybe it had been a heart attack. Maybe she had died of fright. Maybe she'd caught a very bad case of flu. Everyone had their own ideas ... but I knew better. I remembered the twist of silver I had seen on the carpet.

"Tim, what can you tell me about Sylvie Binns?" I asked.

"Not a lot." Tim fell silent. "She was good at chemistry."

"I know that."

"She used to go out with Mark. We always thought the two of them would get married, but in the end she met someone else. Mark ran all the way round England. That was his way of forgetting her."

Mark Tyler had been the last person to see Sylvie alive. I wondered if he really had forgotten her. Or forgiven her.

"Maybe she was ill before she came to the island," Tim muttered.

"Tim, I think she was poisoned," I said.

"Poisoned?"

I remembered my first sight of Sylvie, on the

29

quay. She had been eating a chocolate flake. "Sylvie liked sweets and chocolate," I said.

"You're right, Nick! Yes. She loved chocolate. She could never resist it. When Mark was going out with her, he took her on a tour of a chocolate factory. She even ate the tickets." Tim frowned. "But what's that got to do with anything?"

"There was a piece of silver paper on the floor in her room. I think it was the wrapper off a sweet or a chocolate. Don't you see? Someone knew she couldn't resist chocolate – so they left one in her room. Maybe on her pillow."

"And it wasn't almond crunch," Tim muttered darkly.

"More likely cyanide surprise," I said.

We got into bed. Tim didn't want to turn off the lights, but a few minutes later, after he had dozed off, I reached for the switch and lay back in the darkness. I needed to think. Sylvie had eaten a poisoned chocolate. I was sure of it. But had she been given it or had she found it in her room? If it was already in the room, it could have been left there before we arrived. But if she had been given it, then the killer must still be on the island. He or she might even be in the house.

There was a movement at the window.

At first I thought I'd imagined it, but propping myself up in the bed, I saw it again. There was somebody there! No – that was impossible.

We were on the first floor. Then I remembered. There was a terrace running round the outside of the house, connecting all the bedrooms.

There it was again. I stared in horror. There was a face staring at me from the other side of the glass, a hideous skull with hollow eyes and grinning, tombstone teeth. The bones glowed in the moonlight. Now I'll be honest with you. I don't scare easily. But right then I was frozen. I couldn't move. I couldn't cry out. I'm almost surprised I didn't wet the bed.

The skull hovered in front of me. I couldn't see a body. It had to be draped in black. It's a mask, I told myself. Someone is trying to frighten you with a joke-shop mask. Somehow, I managed to force back the fear. I jerked up in bed and threw back the covers. Next to me, Tim woke up.

"Is it breakfast already?" he asked.

I ignored him. I was already darting towards the window. But at that moment, the moon vanished behind another cloud and the darkness fell. By the time I had found the lock and opened the window, the man – or woman, whoever it was – had gone.

"What is it, Nick?" Tim demanded.

I didn't answer. But it seemed that whoever had killed Rory McDougal and Sylvie Binns was still on the island.

Which left me wondering – who was going to be next?

SEARCH PARTY

Janet Rhodes didn't make it to breakfast.

There were just the five of us, sitting in the kitchen with five bowls of Frosties and a steaming plate of scrambled eggs that Brenda had insisted on cooking but which nobody felt like eating. Libby had another cigarette in her mouth but everyone had complained so much that she wasn't smoking it. She was sucking it. Eric was still in his dressing-gown, a thick red thing with his initials – ED – embroidered on the pocket. Mark was wearing a track suit. A security camera winked at us from one corner of the room. There were a lot of security cameras on the island. But none of us felt even slightly secure.

"What are we going to do?" Brenda asked. I got the feeling that she hadn't slept very much the night before. There were dark rings under her eyes and although she'd put on lipstick, most of it had missed her lips. "This island is haunted!" she went on.

"What do you mean?" Eric asked.

"Last night ... my window ... it was horrible."

"I've got quite a nice window," Tim said.

"I mean ... I saw something! A human skull. It was dancing in the night air."

So she'd seen it too! I was about to chip in, but then Eric interrupted. "I don't think it's going to help, sharing our bad dreams," he said.

"I didn't dream it," Brenda insisted.

"We've got to do something!" Mark cut in. "First Rory, then Sylvie. At this rate, there won't be any of us left by lunch-time."

"I don't want any lunch," Libby muttered.

"We need to talk about this," Eric said. "We need to work something out. But there's no point starting until we're all here." He glanced at the clock. "Where the hell is Janet?"

"Maybe she's in the bath," Tim suggested.

"In the water or underneath it?" Eric growled.

The minute hand on the kitchen clock ticked forward. It was nine o'clock. Suddenly Mark stood up. "I'm going upstairs," he announced.

"You're going back to bed?" Tim asked.

"I'm going to find her."

He left the room. The rest of us followed

33

him, tiptoeing up the stairs and along the corridor with a sense of dread. Actually, Eric didn't exactly tiptoe. He was so fat that it must have been quite a few years since his toes *had* tips. Mark Tyler had moved quickly, taking the stairs four at a time as if they were hurdles and he was back at the Olympic games at Atlanta. He was outside the door when we arrived.

"She's overslept," Tim said to me. "She's fine. She's just overslept."

Eric knocked on her door. There was no answer. He knocked again, then turned the handle. The door opened.

The hairdresser had overslept all right, but nothing was ever going to wake her up again. She had been stabbed during the night. She was lying on her back on a four-poster bed like the one in our room, only smaller. The bed was old. The paint had peeled off the posts and there was a tear in the canopy above her. In fact the whole room looked shabby, as if it had been missed out by the decorators. Maybe I noticed all this because I didn't want to look at the body. You may think I'm crazy, but dead people upset me. And when I did finally look at her, I got a shock.

Whoever had killed her hadn't used a knife. There was something sticking out of her chest and at first I thought it was some sort of rocket. It was silver, in the shape of a sort of long pyramid, with four legs jutting out. Then, slowly, it dawned on me what I was looking at. It was a model, a souvenir of the building that I had climbed up with Tim only the year before.

It was incredible. But true. Janet Rhodes had been stabbed with a model of the Eiffel Tower.

"The Eiffel Tower!" Tim muttered. His face was the colour of sour milk. "It's an outrage. I mean, it's meant to be a tourist attraction!"

"Why the Eiffel Tower?" I asked.

"Because it's famous, Nick. People like to visit it."

"No – I don't mean, why is it a tourist attraction. I mean, why use it as a murder weapon? It's certainly a strange choice. Maybe someone is trying to tell us something."

"Well, they certainly told Janet something," Tim said.

We were back at the breakfast table. The scrambled eggs were cold and congealed and looked even less appetizing than before. All the Frosties had gone soggy. But it didn't matter. There was no way anybody was going to eat anything today. The way things were going, I wondered if any of us would ever eat anything again.

Nobody was talking very much. I knew why. But it was Brenda who put it into words.

"Do you realize…" she began, and for once

her voice was hoarse and empty. "Do you realize that the killer could be sitting here, at this table."

Tim looked around. "But there's only us here!"

"That's what she means, Tim," I said. "She's saying that the killer could be one of us!"

Brenda nodded. "I know it's one of us. One of us got up last night and went down the corridor." She shuddered. "I thought I heard squeaking last night…"

"That was Tim," I said. "He snores."

"No. It was a floorboard. Somebody left their room…"

"Did anyone else hear anything last night?" Eric asked.

There was a pause. Then Libby nodded. "I have the room next to Mark," she said. She turned to look at him. "I heard your door open just after midnight. I heard you go into the corridor."

"I went to the toilet," Mark replied. His dark face had suddenly got darker. He didn't like being accused.

"You went to the toilet in the corridor?" Tim asked.

"I went to the toilet which is across the corridor, opposite my room. I didn't go anywhere near Janet."

"What about the skull?" Brenda whispered.

Eric scowled. He had forgotten about the dancing skull. "I know you say it's a dream, Eric," she went on. "But that's typical of you. You never believed anything I said, even when we were at school. Well, believe me now..." she took a deep breath. "Maybe it wasn't a ghost or a monster. Maybe it was someone in a mask. But they were there! I was awake. I jumped out of bed and went over to the window but by the time I got there, seconds later, they'd gone. Vanished into thin air..."

"It wasn't a dream," I said. "I saw it too."

"You?" Eric sneered at me.

I nodded.

"I didn't see anything," Tim said.

"You were asleep, Tim. But it was definitely there. It came out of nowhere ... like a magic trick. A rabbit out of a hat!"

"You saw a rabbit too?" Tim asked.

We all ignored him. "Any one of us could have climbed out onto the terrace," Brenda said. "Any one of us could have killed Janet. And Rory. And Sylvie! How do we know that she wasn't strangled or poisoned or something?"

"I think she *was* poisoned," I said.

Everyone looked at me so I told them about the sweet wrapper and Sylvie's love of chocolate. It was strange. Everyone in the room was ten years older than me but suddenly I was in control.

Not for long, though. Eric Draper, the ex-head boy, raised his hands. "Ladies and gentlemen," he announced. "I don't think we should jump to conclusions. Why would any of us sitting at this table want to kill Rory or Sylvie or Janet?"

"Mark used to go out with Sylvie," Libby said. She was staring at him. "When she broke up with you, you told me you wanted to kill her."

"That was ten years ago!" Mark protested. He jerked a finger at Libby. "Anyway, what about *you*? You nearly *did* kill Rory with that bicycle pump..."

"Yes. And what about you!" Tim pointed at Eric. "You say your name's Eric, so why are you wearing a dressing-gown that belongs to Ed?"

It took Eric a few seconds to work out what Tim was getting at. "Those are my initials, you idiot!" he snapped. He took a deep breath and raised his hands. "Look," he went on. "There's no point arguing amongst ourselves. We have to stick together. It could be our only hope."

The others fell silent. I had to admit, Eric was speaking sense. Blaming each other wouldn't help.

"Both Brenda and ... Tim's little brother saw somebody last night," he went on. I didn't know why he couldn't call me by my name.

38

"Now that could have been one of us, dressing up to frighten the others. But remember, we were all inside the house ... and this thing, whatever it was, was outside. So maybe it was someone else. Maybe it was someone we don't know about."

"You mean ... someone hiding on the island?" Mark said.

"Exactly. We know we can't call the police. We know we're stuck here. But it seems to me that the first thing we have to do is find out if there's anyone else here."

"We've got to organize a search party," I said.

Tim shook his head. "This is no time for a party, Nick," he muttered.

"You're right, Eric," Libby said. "We've got to go over the island from head to tail."

"But at the same time, I think we should keep an eye on each other," Brenda said. "I'll feel safer that way."

Eric went upstairs to get changed. Mark went with him. From now on, we were going to do everything in pairs. Brenda and Libby cleared the breakfast things. I'd already noticed that most of the food in the house was in tins – which was just as well. Even the cleverest killer couldn't tamper with a tin, so at least we wouldn't starve. At half past nine we all met in the hall. Then we put on our coats and went outside.

The search began back at the jetty, right at the head of the crocodile. The idea was that we could cover the entire island, working like the police searching a wood when someone has gone missing. That is, we kept ten metres apart, always in sight of one another, moving across the island in a line. It was a beautiful day. The sun was shining and the sea was blue, but even so I could feel a chill breeze on Crocodile Island. And there was something else. I couldn't escape the feeling that I was being watched. It was weird. Because it was obvious that there wasn't anybody in sight ... not even so much as a sheep or a cow.

It only took us an hour to cover the island. There really wasn't very much there. Most of it was covered in gorse that only came up to the knee, which no killer could have hidden behind – unless, of course, he happened to be extremely small. There were a few trees but we checked the branches and Tim even climbed one to see if anyone was hiding at the top. Then I climbed up to help Tim down again and we moved on. We came to a couple of ruined outbuildings. I went inside. There was nobody there – but I did see something. Another security camera, fixed to the brickwork. Of course, a rich man like Rory would have had to be careful about security. I remembered the camera I had noticed in the kitchen. He had probably covered the whole island. Was that why I had felt we were being watched?

We went past the house and continued towards the crocodile's tail. The ground rose steeply up, finally arriving at a narrow point at least twenty metres above the sea. This was what I had seen from the boat. Six great rocks, steel grey and needle-sharp, rose out of the water far below. Looking down made my head spin. I wondered briefly if there might be a cave somewhere, perhaps tucked underneath the lip where we were standing. But then a wave rolled in, crashing against the cliff face. If there was a killer down there, he'd be soaking wet. And anyway, as far as I could see, there was no way down.

We moved away, retracing our steps. There was nobody outside the house, but how about inside? Starting in the hall, we went from room to room: the library, the dining-room, the conservatory, the hall and so on. We looked behind curtains, under tables, in the fireplaces and up the chimneys. Tim even looked in the grandfather clocks. Maybe he thought he'd find somebody's grandfather. We covered the ground floor and then went up to the first. Here were the bedrooms, with our names still attached to the doors. We went into every one of them. There was nobody there ... apart from the three very dead bodies. It wasn't easy searching those particular rooms, but we made ourselves ... although I think Tim was wasting his time doing it with his eyes tightly shut.

Nobody in the rooms. Nobody in the corridors. We found the attic but all that was there was a water tank. Tim dipped his head in and I made a mental note not to drink any more water. Not with his dandruff. Eventually, we gave up. We had been everywhere. There was nowhere else to look.

We started to go back down to the kitchen but had only got halfway there when Libby let out a little gasp.

"What is it?" Eric demanded.

"There." She pointed at the wall at the end of the corridor. "I don't know why I didn't see it before!"

What she had seen was a black-and-white photograph in a silver frame. It was hanging right in the middle of the wall with enough space around it to make it stand out. The question was – had Rory hung it there? Or had it been someone else? Was this something we were meant to see?

The photograph showed nine teenagers, all of them wearing the same uniform. It's funny how people change in ten years – but I recognized them at once: Eric Draper, Janet Rhodes, Mark Tyler, Brenda Blake, Sylvie Binns, Libby Goldman, Rory McDougal and Tim. Tim looked the weirdest of them all. He'd had long hair then, and spots. Lots of spots. Of course, I wouldn't have looked too great myself when the picture had been taken – but then I would only have been four years old.

There was one face, however, that I didn't know. He was standing at the edge of the group, slightly apart; a thin, gangly teenager with curly hair and glasses. He was wearing an anorak and had the sort of face you'd expect to see on a train-spotter. "Who's he?" I asked.

"That's Johnny!" Brenda replied. "Johnny Nadler. He was one of my best friends…"

"And mine," Libby agreed. "Everyone liked Johnny. We used to hang out with him in the yard." She walked closer to the photograph. "I remember when this was taken. It was prize-giving day. He came second in geography. I came first."

"Wait a minute," I interrupted. "Everyone in this photograph is here on Crocodile Island. Everyone except Johnny Nadler!"

"You're right!" Mark agreed. "Why wasn't he invited?"

"Because he's the killer!" Eric snapped. "He's got to be!"

"But why would Johnny want to kill Rory?" Brenda asked. "The two of them were friends. And every day after school he used to catch the bus with Sylvie – even though it took him eight miles in the wrong direction. That's how much he liked her."

"He let Janet cut his hair," Libby went on. "She accidentally cut a chunk out of his ear, but he didn't mind. In fact he laughed all the way to the hospital. Johnny wouldn't hurt anyone."

"What else can you tell me about him?" I asked.

"He came second in history as well as geography," Eric said. "He was really clever."

"He was always playing with model planes and cars," Mark added. "He used to build them himself. We always said he'd be an inventor when he left school but in fact he ended up working at Boots. I saw him there once, when I went in to get some ointment." He blushed. "I had athlete's foot."

"Did any of the rest of you ever see him again?" I asked.

Everyone shook their heads. I looked at the photograph again. It did seem strange that he was the only one in the picture who hadn't been invited to Crocodile Island. But did that make him the killer? And if so, where on earth was he? We had searched the entire island and we were certain now that we were the only ones who were there.

Eric looked at his watch. It was half past twelve. "I suggest we continue this meeting downstairs," he said.

"I need to change," Brenda said.

"Me too," Libby agreed.

Everyone started to move in different directions.

"Hold on a minute!" I said. "I thought we were all going to stick together. I think we should all stay in this room."

"Don't be ridiculous!" Eric snapped. "We have to eat something. It's lunch-time. And anyway, we've just searched the island. We know there's nobody else here."

"Well, I'm staying with Tim," I said.

"How do you know I'm not the killer?" Tim demanded.

Because whoever killed Rory and the others is brilliant and fiendish and you still have trouble tying your shoelaces. That was what I thought, but I didn't say anything. I just shrugged.

"I don't want to be near anyone," Libby said. "I feel safer on my own."

"Me too." Brenda nodded. "And I'm certainly not having anyone in the room with me while I'm changing."

"We can meet in ten minutes," Eric said. "We're inside the house. We know there's nobody else on the island. We'll meet in the dining-room at twenty to one."

He was wrong of course. This was one little group that was never going to meet again. But how could we know that? We were scared and we weren't thinking straight.

Tim and I went back to our room. Tim scratched his head, which was still damp from the water tank. "Johnny could be hiding on

45

the island," he said. "What if there's a secret room?"

The same thought had already occurred to me, but I'd tapped every wall and every wooden panel and nothing had sounded hollow. "I don't think there are any secret rooms, Tim," I said.

"But you can't be sure…" Tim began to tap his way along the wall, his eyes half-closed, listening for a hollow sound. A few moments later, he straightened up, excited. "There's definitely something on the other side here!" he cried.

"I know, Tim," I said. "That's the window."

I left him in the bedroom, drying his hair, and went back downstairs. I was going to join the others in the dining-room. But I never got that far. I was about halfway down when I heard it. A short, sudden scream. Then a crashing sound. It had come from somewhere outside.

I ran down the rest of the way, through the hall and out the front door. Mark Tyler appeared, running round the side of the house.

"What was it…?" he demanded. He was trying not to sound scared but it wasn't working.

"Round the back?"

We went there together, moving more slowly now, knowing what we were going to find, not wanting to find it. The kitchen door opened and Brenda Blake came out. I noticed she was breathing heavily.

This time it was Libby Goldman. I'm afraid she had recorded her last episode of *Libby's Lounge* and for her the final credits were already rolling. Why had she gone outside? Maybe she'd decided to light up one of her cigarettes – in which case, this was one time when smoking certainly had been bad for her health. Fatal, in fact. But it hadn't been the tobacco that had killed her. Something had hit her hard on the head: something that had been dropped from above. I looked up, working out the angles. We were directly underneath the battlements. Behind them, the roof was flat. It would have been easy enough for someone to hide up there, to wait for any one of us to step outside. Libby must have come out to get a breath of fresh air before the meeting. Air wasn't something she'd be needing again.

There were footsteps on the gravel. Eric and Tim had arrived. They stared in silence. Mark stretched out a finger and pointed. It took me a minute to work out what he was pointing at. That was how much his finger was trembling.

And there it was, lying in the grass. At first I didn't recognize the object that had been dropped from the roof and which had fallen right onto Libby Goldman. I mean, I knew what it was – but I couldn't believe that that was what had been used.

It was a big round ball: a globe. The sort of thing you find in a library. Maybe it had been in Rory's library before the killer had carried it up to the roof. The United States of America was facing up. It was stained red.

I looked at Eric Draper. His mouth had dropped open. He looked genuinely shocked. Mark Tyler was standing opposite him, staring. Brenda Blake was to one side. She was crying.

One of them had to be faking it. I was certain of it. One of them had to have climbed down from the room after watching Libby fall. There was nobody else here. One of them had to be the killer.

But which one?

MORE MURDER

Eric Draper? Brenda Blake? Or Mark Tyler?

It was early evening and Tim and I had gone for a walk – supposedly to clear our heads. But the truth was, I wanted to be alone with him and somehow I felt safer away from the house. It struck me that all the deaths had taken place inside or near the building. And if we stayed too close to the house something else might strike me – a falling piano or a model of the Taj Mahal, for example.

I glanced down at the piece of paper I was holding in my hand. I had made a few notes just before we left:

RORY McDOUGAL – Killed with a sword.
SYLVIE BINNS – Poisoned.
JANET RHODES – Stabbed with an Eiffel Tower!

LIBBY GOLDMAN – Knocked down with a globe.

There was a pattern in there somewhere but I just couldn't see it. Maybe some fresh air would help after all.

"I've got an idea!" Tim said.

"Go ahead, Tim," I said.

"Maybe I could swim back over to the coast and get some help."

We were sitting on the jetty. Today the sea was flat, the waves caught as if in a photograph. I could just make out the mainland, a vague ribbon lying on the horizon. The sun was setting fast. How many of us would see it rise again?

I shook my head. "No, Tim. It's too far."

"It can't be more than five miles."

"And you can't swim."

"Oh yes. I'd forgotten." He glanced at me. "But you can."

"I can't swim five miles!" I said. "The water's too cold. And there's too much of it. No. Our only hope is to solve this before the killer strikes again."

"You're right, Nick." Tim closed his eyes and sat in silence for a minute. Then he opened them again. "Maybe we could get one of the others to swim…"

"One of the others *is* the killer!" I said. "I saw someone out on the terrace, wearing a

skeleton mask. I don't know how they managed to disappear so quickly – but I wasn't
imagining it. Brenda saw them too."

"Maybe it was Mark! He's a fast mover."

"And just now … when Libby Goldman was
killed. Someone must have climbed up onto the
roof." I thought back. "Brenda was out of
breath when she came into the garden…"

"She could have been singing!"

"I doubt it. But she could have been running. She drops the globe, then runs all the
way downstairs…"

A seagull flew overhead, crying mournfully.
I knew how it felt. I almost wanted to cry
myself.

"What's missing is the motive," I went on.
"Think back, Tim. You were at school with
these people. There are only three of them left
– Brenda, Mark and Eric. Would any of them
have any reason to kill the rest of you?"

Tim sighed. "The only people who ever
threatened to kill me," he said, "were the
teachers. My French teacher once threw a
piece of chalk at me. And when that missed, he
threw the blackboard."

"How did you get on with Mark Tyler?"

"We were friends. We used to play conkers
together." He scratched his head. "I did once
miss his conker and break three of his fingers,
but I don't think he minded too much."

"How about Brenda Blake?"

Tim thought back. "She was in the school choir," he said. "She was also in the rugby team. She used to sing in the scrum." He scratched his head. "We used to tease her a bit but it was never serious."

"Maybe she didn't agree."

The waves rolled in towards us. I looked out at the mainland, hoping to catch sight of Horatio Randle and his boat, the *Silver Medal*. But the sea was empty, darkening as the sun dipped behind it. What had the old fisherman said when he'd dropped us? *"I'll be back in a couple of days."* It had been Wednesday when we arrived. He might not return until the weekend. How many passengers would there be left waiting for him?

"How about Eric Draper?" I asked.

"What about him?"

"He could be the killer. It would have to be someone strong to carry the globe up to the roof in the first place. Can you remember anything about him?"

Tim laughed. "He was a great sport. I'll never forget the last day of term when the seven of us pulled off his trousers and threw him in the canal!"

"What?" I exclaimed. "You pulled off his trousers and threw him in the canal? Why?"

"Well, he was the head boy. And he'd always been bossy. It was just a bit of fun. Except that he nearly drowned. And the canal was so polluted, he had to spend six months in hospital."

"Are you telling me that the seven of you nearly killed Eric?" I was almost screaming. "Hasn't it occurred to you that this whole thing could be his revenge?"

"But it was just a joke!"

"You almost killed him, Tim! Maybe he wasn't amused."

I stood up. It was time to go back to the house. The other three would be waiting for us … if they'd managed to survive the last half-hour.

"I wish I'd never come here," Tim muttered.

"I wish you'd never come here," I agreed.

"Poor Libby. And Sylvie. And Janet. And Rory, of course. He was first."

We walked a few more steps in silence. Then I suddenly stopped. "What did you say, Tim?" I demanded.

"I didn't say anything!"

"Yes, you did! Before you weren't saying anything, you were saying something."

"I asked which side of the bed you wanted."

"No. That was yesterday." I played back what he had just said and that was when I saw it, the pattern I'd been looking for. "You're brilliant!" I said.

"Thanks!" Tim frowned. "What have I done?"

"Tell me," I said. "Did Libby come first in

anything at school? And was it ... by any chance ... geography?"

"Yes. She did. How did you know?"

"Let's get back inside," I said.

I found Eric, Mark and Brenda in the drawing-room. This was one of the most extraordinary rooms in the house – almost like a chapel with a great stained glass window at one end and a high, vaulted ceiling. Rory McDougal had obviously fancied himself as a musician. There was even a church organ against the wall, the silver pipes looming over us. Like so many of the other rooms, the walls were lined with old weapons. In here they were antique pistols; muskets and flintlocks. All in all, we couldn't have chosen a worse house to share with a mass murderer. There were more weapons than you'd find in the Tower of London and I just hoped that they weren't as real as they looked.

The three survivors were sitting in heavy, leather chairs. I stood in front of them with the organ on one side and a row of bookshelves on the other. Everyone was watching me and I felt a bit like Hercule Poirot at the end of one of his cases, explaining it to the suspects. The only trouble was, this wasn't the end of the case. I was still certain that I was talking to the murderer. He or she had to be one of the people in the room.

Somewhere outside, a clock chimed the

hour. It was nine o'clock. Night had fallen.

"Seven of you were invited to Crocodile Island," I began. "And I see now that you all have something in common."

"We went to the same school," interrupted Tim.

"I know that, Tim. But there's something else. You all got prizes for coming first. You've already told me that Rory was first in maths. Libby was first in geography..."

"What's this got to do with anything?" Eric snapped.

"Don't you see? Libby was first in geography and someone dropped a globe on her head. Someone told me that Sylvie Binns came first in chemistry and we think she was poisoned."

"Janet came first in French..." Mark murmured.

"...which would explain why she was stabbed with a model of the Eiffel Tower. And Rory McDougal came first in maths."

"He was stabbed too," Eric said.

"He was more than stabbed. He was divided!"

There was a long silence.

"That's the reason why Johnny Nadler wasn't invited to the island," Brenda said. "He never came first in anything. He was second..."

"But that means..." Eric had gone pale. "I came first in history."

"I came first in sport," Mark said.

Brenda nodded. "And I came first in music."

We all turned to look at Tim. But he couldn't have come first in anything ... could he? I noticed he was blushing. He licked his lips and looked the other way.

"What did you come first in, Tim?" I asked.

"I didn't..." he began, but I could tell he was lying.

"We have to know," I said. "It could be important."

"I remember..." Brenda began.

"All right," Tim sighed. "I got first prize in needlework."

"Needlework!" I exclaimed.

"Well ... yes. It was a hobby of mine. Just for a bit. I mean..." He was going redder and redder. "I didn't even want the prize. I just got it. It was for a handkerchief..."

The idea of my sixteen-year-old brother winning a prize for an embroidered hanky made my head spin. But this wasn't the time to laugh. Hopefully I'd be able to do that later.

"Wait a minute! Wait a minute!" Eric said. He looked annoyed. Maybe it was because I was ten years younger than him and I was the one who'd worked it out. "I came first in history – and you're saying I'm going to be killed ... *historically*?"

"That's what it looks like," I said.

"But how...?"

I pointed at the wall, at the flintlock pistols on the wooden plaques. "Maybe someone will use one of those," I said. "Or there are swords, arrows, spears ... that bear upstairs is even holding a blunderbuss. This place is full of old weapons."

"What about me?" Brenda whispered.

"You're not an old weapon!" Tim said.

"I came first in music." Brenda glared at the organ as if it was about to jump off the wall and eat her.

"But who's *doing* this?" Mark cut in. "I mean ... it's got to be someone in this room. Right? We know there's nobody else on the island. There can't be anybody hiding. We've searched everywhere."

"It's him!" Brenda pointed at Eric. "He never forgave us for throwing him in the canal. This is his revenge!"

"What about *you*?" Eric returned. "You once said you were going to kill us all. It was in the school yard. I remember it clearly!"

"That's true!" Mark said.

"You used to bully me all the time," Brenda wailed. "Just because I had pigtails. And crooked teeth."

"And you were fat," Tim reminded her.

"But I didn't mean it, when I said that." She turned to Mark. "You said you were going to kill Tim when he broke all your fingers with that conker!"

"I only broke three of them!" Tim interrupted.

"I didn't much like Tim," Mark agreed. "And you're right. I would have quite happily strangled him. Not that it would have been easy with three broken fingers. But I never had any argument with you or with Eric or any of the others. Why would I want to kill you?"

"It's still got to be one of us," Eric insisted. He paused. "It can't be Tim," he went on.

"Why not?" Tim asked.

"Because this whole business is the work of a fiendish madman and you're not fiendish. You're just silly!"

"Oh thanks!" Tim looked away.

"I know it's not me..." Eric went on.

"That's what you say," Brenda sniffed.

"I know it's not me, so it's got to be Brenda or Mark."

"What about Sylvie?" Tim suggested.

"She's already dead, Tim," I reminded him, quietly.

"Oh yes."

"This is all irrelevant," Mark said. "The question is – what are we going to do? We could be stuck on this island for days, or even weeks. It all depends on when Captain Randle comes back. And by then it could be too late!"

"I'd like to make a suggestion," I said. Everyone stopped and looked at me. "The first thing is, we've all got to keep each other in sight."

"The kid's right," Mark agreed. "So long as we can see each other, we're going to be safe."

"That's true!" Tim exclaimed. "All we have to do is keep our eyes open and everything will be fine." He turned to me. "You're brilliant, Nick. For a moment there I was getting really worried."

Then all the lights went out.

It happened so suddenly that for a moment I thought it was just me. Had I been knocked out or somehow closed my eyes without noticing? The last thing I saw was the four of them – Eric, Brenda, Mark and Tim – sitting in their chairs as if caught in a photograph. Then everything was black. There was no moon that night and even if there had been the stained glass window would have kept most of the light out. Darkness came crashing onto us. It was total.

"Don't panic!" Eric said.

There was a gunshot. I saw it, a spark of red on the other side of the room.

Tim screamed and for a horrible moment I wondered if he had been shot. I forced myself to calm down. He'd come first in needlework. Nobody would be aiming a gun at him.

"Tim!" I called out.

"Can I panic now?" he called back.

"Eric...?" That was Mark's voice.

And then there was a sort of groaning sound, followed by a heavy thud. At the same time I heard a door open and close. I stood up, trying to see through the darkness. But it was hopeless. I couldn't even make out my own hand in front of my face.

"Tim?" I called again.

"Nick?" I was relieved to hear his voice.

"Eric?" I tried.

Silence.

"Brenda?"

Nothing.

"Mark?"

The lights came back on.

There were only two people alive in the room. I was standing in front of my chair. One more step and I'd have put my foot through the coffee table. Tim was *under* the coffee table. He must have crawled there when the lights went out. Eric was on the floor. He had been shot. There was a flintlock pistol, still smoking, lying on the carpet on the other side of the room. It must have been taken off the wall, fired and then dropped. At least, that's what it looked like. Brenda was sitting in her chair. She was dead too. One of the organ pipes – the largest – had been pulled down on top of her. That must have been the thud I had heard. Brenda had sung her last opera. The only music she needed now was a hymn.

There was no sign of Mark.

"Are you all right, Tim?" I demanded.

"Yes!" Tim sounded surprised. "I haven't been murdered!" he exclaimed.

"I noticed." I waited while he climbed out from underneath the coffee table. "At least we know who the killer is," I said.

"Do we?"

"It's got to be Mark." I said. "Mark Tyler..."

"I always knew it was him," Tim said. "Call it intuition. Call it experience. But I knew he was a killer even before he'd done any killing."

"I don't know, Tim," I said. It bothered me, because to be honest Mark was the last person I would have suspected. And yet, at the same time, I had to admit ... it would have taken a fast mover to push the globe off the roof and make it all the way downstairs in time and Mark was the fastest person on the island.

"Where do you think he went?" Tim asked.

"I don't know."

We left the room carefully. In fact, Tim made me leave it first. The fact was that – unless I'd got the whole thing wrong – it was just the three of us now on the island; Mark could be waiting for us anywhere. Or waiting for Tim, rather. He had no quarrel with me. And that made me think. Tim had come first in needlework. Following the pattern of the other deaths, that meant he would probably be

61

killed with some sort of needle. But what would that mean? A sewing needle dipped in poison? A hypodermic syringe?

Tim must have had the same thought. He was looking everywhere, afraid to touch anything, afraid even to take another step. We went out into the hall. The fire had died down and was glowing red. The front door was open.

"Maybe he went outside," Tim said.

"What would be the point?" I asked.

Tim shuddered. "Don't talk about points," he said.

We went outside. And that was where we found Mark. He had come first in sport but now he had reached the finishing line. Somebody had been throwing the javelin and they'd thrown it at him. It had hit him in the chest. He was lying on the grass, doing a good impersonation of a sausage on a stick.

"It's ... it's ... it's..." Tim couldn't finish the sentence.

"Yeah," I said. "It's Mark." There were a few leaves scattered around his body. That puzzled me. The nearest trees were ten metres away. But this wasn't the time to play the detective. There were no more suspects. And only one more victim.

I looked at Tim.

Tim looked at me.

We were the only two left.

NEEDLES

Tim didn't sleep well that night. Although I hadn't said anything, not wanting to upset him, even he had managed to work out that he had to be the next on the killer's list. He also knew that his own murder would have something to do with needlework. So he was looking for needles everywhere.

By one o'clock in the morning we knew that there were no sewing needles in the room, no knitting needles and no pine needles. Even so, it took him an hour to get into bed and several more hours to get to sleep. Mind you, nobody would have found it easy getting to sleep dressed in a full suit of medieval armour, but that still hadn't stopped Tim putting it on.

"There could be a poisoned needle in the mattress," he said. "Or someone could try and inject me with a syringe."

Tim didn't snore that night; he clanked.

Every time he rolled over he sounded like twenty cans of beans in a washing machine. I just hoped he wasn't planning to take a bath in the suit of armour the following morning. That way he could end up rusting to death.

At four-thirty, he woke up screaming.

"What is it, Tim?" I asked.

"I had a bad dream, Nick," he said.

"Don't tell me. You saw a needle."

"No. I saw a haystack."

I didn't sleep well either. I got cramp and woke up in the morning with pins and needles. I didn't tell Tim, though. He'd have had a fit.

We had breakfast together in the kitchen. Neither of us ate very much. For a start, we were surrounded by dead bodies, which didn't make us feel exactly cheerful. But Tim was also terrified. I'd managed to persuade him to change out of the armour but now he was worrying about the food. Were there going to be needles in the cereal? A needle in the tea? In the end, I gave him a straw with a tissue sellotaped over the end. The tissue worked as a filter and he was able to suck up a little orange juice and a very softly-boiled egg.

I have to say that for once I was baffled. It was still like being in an Agatha Christie novel – only this time I couldn't flick through to the last page and see who did it without bothering to read the rest. Personally, I had always thought Eric had been the killer. He seemed to have the strongest motive – being half-drowned on the last day of school. It was funny really. All eight of the old boys and girls of St Egbert's had disliked each other. But someone, somewhere, had disliked them all even more. The whole thing had been planned right down to the last detail. And the last detail, unfortunately, was Tim.

But who? And why?

Tim sat miserably at his end of the table, hardly daring to move. Why had he had to come first in *needlework* of all things? How was I supposed to find the needle that was going to kill him? I knew now that the only hope for me was to solve this thing before the killer struck one last time. And a nasty thought had already occurred to me. Would the killer stop with Tim? I wasn't meant to be part of this. I had never gone to St Egbert's. But I was a witness to what had happened and maybe I had seen too much.

I went over what had happened last night. We had always assumed that there was nobody else on the island, but thinking it through I knew this couldn't be true. We had all been sitting down: Brenda in front of the organ, Eric opposite her, Mark nearest the door and Tim and me on the sofa. But none of us had been anywhere near the light switch, and someone had most certainly turned off the lights – not just in the drawing-room but throughout the entire house. Somewhere down in the basement, there would be a main fuse switch. But that led to another question. If the killer had been down in the basement, then how had he or she managed to appear in the room seconds later to shoot Eric and push the organ pipe onto Brenda?

At the time, I had assumed that Mark had committed the last two murders. There had been a shot, then a thud, then the opening and closing of a door. But a few seconds later, Mark had himself been killed. And what about the leaves that I had seen lying next to his body? How had they got there?

I thought back to the other murders. Rory first. We had all been on the island and we had all separated. Any one of us could have attacked him and, immediately afterwards, left the chocolate on the bed for Sylvie to find. That was the night I had seen the face at the window. A face that had appeared and disappeared – impossibly – in seconds. And then we had found Janet. I remembered her lying in her bed, stabbed by a model of the Eiffel Tower. Her room had been shabby. There had been a tear in the canopy ... I had remarked on it at the time. Why had it caught my eye?

Libby Goldman next. The television presenter had been knocked down with a model globe. There was something strange about that, too. Someone must have carried it up to the roof and dropped it on her when she came out of the front door. But now that I thought about it, I hadn't seen the globe in any of the rooms when we had been searching the house. And that could only mean one thing. It had been on the roof from the very start, waiting for her...

Maybe you know how it is when you've been given a particularly nasty piece of homework – an impossible equation or a fiendish bit of physics or something. You stare at it and stare at it, but it's all just ink on paper and you're about to give up when you notice something and suddenly you realize it's not so difficult after all. Well, that was what was happening to me now.

I remembered the search party, slowly crisscrossing the island. We had seen security cameras everywhere and from the day I had arrived, I had felt that I was being watched. There was a security camera in the kitchen. I looked up. It was watching me even now. Were there cameras in other rooms, too?

At the same time, I remembered something Mark had said, when we had found the old photograph of St Egbert's. And in that second, as quickly as that, I suddenly knew everything.

"I've got it, Tim!" I said.

"So have I, Nick!" Tim cried.

I'd been so wrapped up in my own thoughts, that I hadn't noticed Tim had been thinking too. Now he was staring at me with the sort of look you see on a fish when it's spent too long out of water.

"You know who did it?" I asked.

"Yes."

"Go on!"

"It's simple!" Tim explained. "First there were eight of us on the island, then seven, then six, then five…"

"I know," I interrupted. "I can count backwards."

"Well, now there are only two of us left. I know it wasn't me who committed the murders." He reached forward and snatched up a spoon. Then he realized what he'd done, put it down and snatched up a knife. He waved it at me. "So the killer must be you!" he exclaimed.

"What?" I couldn't believe what I was hearing.

"There's only us left. You and me. I know it wasn't me so it must have been you."

"But why would I want to kill everyone?" I demanded.

"You tell me!"

"I wouldn't! And I didn't! Don't be ridiculous, Tim."

I stood up. That was a mistake.

"Don't come near me!" Tim yelled, and suddenly he sprang out of his chair and jumped out of the window. This was an impressive feat. The window wasn't even open.

I couldn't believe what had happened. I knew Tim was stupid but this was remarkable even by his standards. Maybe sleeping in a suit of armour had done something to that tiny organism he called his brain. At the same time, I was suddenly worried. I knew who the killer was now and I knew who was lined up to be the next victim. Tim was outside the house, on his own. He had made himself into a perfect target.

I had no choice. I went after him, jumping through the shattered window. I could see Tim a short distance away, running towards the tail of Crocodile Island. I had no idea where he was going. But nor of course did he. He was panicking – just trying to put as much distance between the two of us as he could. Not easy considering he was trapped on a small island.

"Tim!" I called.

He didn't stop. I ran after him, following the path as it began to climb steeply up towards the cliffs. This was where the island tapered to a point. I slowed down. Tim had already reached the far end. He had nowhere else to go.

The wind blew his hair around his head as he turned to face me. He was still holding the knife. I noticed now that it was a butter knife. If he stabbed me with all his strength he might just manage to give me a small bruise. His face was pale and his eyes were wide open and staring. The last time I had seen him like this was when they had shown *Jurassic Park* on TV.

"Get back, Nick!" he yelled. It was hard to hear him above the crash of the waves.

"You're crazy, Tim!" I called back. "Why would I want to hurt you? I'm your brother. Think about all the adventures we've had together! I've saved your life lots of times." I thought of telling him that I loved him but he'd have known that wasn't true. "I quite like you!" I said. "You've looked after me ever since Mum and Dad emigrated to Australia. We've had fun together!"

Tim hesitated. I could see the doubt in his eyes. He lowered the butter knife. A huge wave rolled in and crashed against the rocks, spraying us both with freezing, salt water. I looked past Tim at the rocks, an idea forming in my mind. There were six iron grey rocks, jutting out of the sea. I had noticed them the day we had searched the island. And of course, rocks like that have a name. Long and slender with pointed tops, standing upright in the water...

They're called needles.

I'm not exactly sure what happened next but I do know that it all happened at the same time.

There was a soft explosion, just where Tim was standing. The earth underneath his feet seemed to separate, falling away.

Tim screamed and his arm jerked. The butter knife spun in the air, the sun glinting off the blade.

I yelled out and threw myself forward. Somehow my hands managed to grab hold of Tim's shirt.

"Don't kill me!" Tim whimpered.

"I'm not killing you, you idiot!" I yelled. "I'm saving you!"

We rolled back together, away from the edge of the cliff ... an edge that was now several centimetres closer to us than it had been seconds before. I was dazed and there was grass in my mouth, but I realized that the killer had struck again. There had been a small explosive charge buried in the ground at the end of the cliff. Someone had detonated it and if I hadn't managed to grab hold of Tim, he would have fallen down towards to the sea, only to crash onto the needles fifty metres below.

We lay on the grass, panting. The sun was beating down on us. It was difficult to see. But then I became aware of a shadow moving towards us. I rolled over and looked up at the figure, limping towards us, a radio transmitter in one hand and a gun in the other.

"Well, well, well," he said. "It looks as if my little plan has finally come unstuck. And just when everything was going so well, too!"

Tim stared at the man. At his single eye, his

single leg, his huge beard. "It's... it's..." he began.

"It's Horatio Randle," I said. "Captain of the *Silver Medal*, the boat that brought us here."

"You got it in one, young lad!" he said.

"But that's not his real name," I went on. "Randle is an anagram. If you switch around the letters, you get..."

"Endral!" Tim exclaimed.

"Nadler," I said. "I think this must be Johnny Nadler. Your old school friend from St Egbert's."

The captain put down the radio transmitter. He had used it, of course, to set off the explosive charge a few moments before. He didn't let go of the gun. With his free hand, he reached up and pulled off the fake beard, the wig and the eye patch. At the same time, he twisted round and released the leg that he'd had tied up behind his back. It only took a few seconds but at once I recognized the thin-faced teenager I had seen in the photograph.

"It seems you've worked it all out," he muttered. His accent had changed too. He was no longer the jolly captain. He was a killer. And he was mad.

"Yes," I said.

"But it's impossible!" Tim burbled. "He couldn't have killed all the others. We looked! There was nobody else on the island!"

"It was Nadler all along," I said. I glanced

at him. The wind raced past and the waves crashed down.

He smiled. "Do go on," he snarled.

"I know what you did," I said. "Last Wednesday, you met us all at the quay, disguised as a captain. You'd sent everyone invitations to this reunion on the island and you even offered to pay a thousand pounds to make sure that they'd all come. Rory McDougal had nothing to do with it, of course. You'd killed him before we even set sail."

"That's right," Nadler said. He was smiling now. There was something horrible about that smile. He was sure this was one story I wouldn't be telling anyone else.

"You killed Rory and you left the poisoned chocolate for Sylvie. Then you dropped us on the island and sailed away again. There was no need for you to stay. Everything was already prepared."

"Are you saying … he wasn't here when he killed everyone?" Tim asked. He was still lying on the grass. There was a buttercup lodged behind his ear.

"That's right. Don't you remember what Mark told us when we were looking at the picture? He said that Johnny Nadler wanted to be an inventor when he left school. He said he was always playing with planes and cars." I glanced at the transmitter lying on the ground just a few feet away. "I assume they were

73

radio-controlled planes and cars," I said.

"That's right!" Tim said. "He was brilliant, Nick! He once landed a helicopter on the science teacher's head!"

"Well, that's how he killed everyone on the island – after he'd finished with Rory McDougal and Sylvie Binns." I took a deep breath, wondering if there was anything I could do. Tim was right next to the edge of the cliff. I was a couple of metres in front of him. We were both lying down. Nadler was standing over us, aiming with the gun. If we so much as moved, he could shoot us both. I had to keep talking and hope that I might somehow find a way to distract him.

"Janet Rhodes was stabbed with an Eiffel Tower," I went on. "But I noticed that there was a tear in the canopy above her bed. I should have put two and two together and realized that the Eiffel Tower was always there, above the bed. It must have been mounted on some sort of spring mechanism. Nadler knew that was where she'd be sleeping. All he had to do was press a button and send the model plunging down. He was probably miles away when he killed her."

"That's right!" Nadler giggled. "I was back on the mainland. I was nowhere near!"

"But what about the face you saw?" Tim asked. "The skull at the window! Brenda saw it too!"

"You've already answered that one, Tim," I said. "A remote control helicopter or something with a mask hanging underneath. Nadler controlled that too. It was easy!"

"But how could he see us?"

I glanced at Nadler and he nodded. He was happy for me to explain how it had been done.

"The whole island is covered in cameras," I said. "That was Rory's security system. We've been watched from the moment we arrived. Nadler knew where we were every minute of the day."

"Right again!" Nadler grinned. He was pleased with himself, I could see that. "It was easy to hack into McDougal's security system and redirect the pictures to my own TV monitor. I was even able to watch you in the bath!"

"That's outrageous!" Tim was blushing. He knew that Nadler would have seen him playing with his plastic duck.

"Nadler had positioned the globe up on the roof," I went on. "If we'd gone up and looked we'd probably have found some sort of ramp with a simple switch. He waited until Libby Goldman came out of the front door and then he pressed the button that released the globe. It rolled forward and that was that. She never had a chance. He killed Eric and Brenda the same way. First he turned out the lights. Then he fired a bullet and brought down an organ pipe ... both by remote control." I paused.

"How about Mark Tyler?" I asked.

"The javelin was hidden in the branches of a tree," Nadler explained. "It was on a giant elastic band. Remote control again. It was just like a crossbow." He giggled for a second time. "Only bigger."

Well that explained the leaves. Some of them must have travelled with the javelin when it was fired.

"And that just left you, Tim," I said. "Nadler had to wait until you came out here. Then he was going to blow the ground out from beneath your feet and watch you fall onto the needles below. And with you dead, his revenge would be complete."

"Revenge?" Tim was genuinely puzzled. "But why did he want revenge? We never did anything to him!"

"I think it was because he came second," I said. I turned to Nadler. "You came second in every subject at school. And the boat you picked us up in. It was called the *Silver Medal*. I guess you chose the name on purpose. Because that's what you're given when you come second."

"That's right." Nadler nodded and now his face had darkened and his lips were twisted into an expression of pain. His finger tightened on the trigger and he looked at me with hatred in his eyes. "I came second in maths, second in chemistry, second in French, second in geography, second in history, second in music and second in sport. I even came second in needlework, even though my embroidered tea towel was much more beautiful than your brother's stupid handkerchief!"

"It was a lovely handkerchief!" Tim said.

"Shut up!" Nadler screamed and for a moment I was afraid he was going to shoot Tim then and there. "Do you have any idea how horrible it is coming second?" he went on. Saliva flecked at his lips. The hand with the gun never moved. "Coming last doesn't matter. Coming fifth or sixth … who cares? But when you come second, everyone knows. You've just missed! You've missed getting the prize by just a few marks. And everyone feels sorry for you. Poor old Johnny! He couldn't quite make it. He wasn't quite good enough."

He took a deep breath. "I've been coming second all my life. I go for jobs and I get down to the last two in the interviews but it's always the other person who gets it. I went out with a girl but then she decided to marry someone else because as far as she was concerned, I was Number Two. When I've tried to sell my inventions, I've discovered that someone else has always got there first. Number Two! Number Two! Number Two! I hate being Number Two…!

"And it's all your fault!" He pointed the gun at Tim and now the fury was back in his eyes. "It all started at St Egbert's! That hateful school! That was where I started coming second and that was why I decided to have my revenge. You all thought you were clever beating me at everything. Well, I've showed you! I've killed the whole lot of you and I've done it in exactly the way you deserve!"

"You haven't killed me!" Tim exclaimed.

I didn't think it was a good idea to point this out. Nadler steadied the gun. "I'm going to do that now," he said. "Your body will still end up smashing into the needles so everything will have worked out the way it was meant to." He nodded at me. "I'll have to kill you too, of course," he continued. "You weren't meant to be here, but I don't mind. You sound too clever for your own good. I'm going to enjoy killing you too!"

He took aim.

"No!" I shouted.

He fired at Tim.

"Missed!" Tim laughed and rolled to one side. He was still laughing when he rolled over the side of the cliff.

"Tim!" I yelled.

"Now it's your turn," Nadler said.

I closed my eyes. There was nothing I could do.

There was a long pause. I opened them again.

Nadler was still standing, but even as I

watched he crumpled to the ground. Eric Draper, the fat solicitor, was standing behind him. There was blood all over his shirt and he was deathly pale. But he was still alive. He was holding the blunderbuss, which he must have taken from the bear. He hadn't fired it. He had used it like a club and knocked Nadler out.

"He only wounded me…" he gasped. "I woke up this morning. I came to find you…"

But I wasn't interested in Eric Draper, even if he had just saved my life. I crawled over to the cliff edge and looked down, expecting to see Tim, smashed to pieces, on the rocks below.

"Hello, Nick!" Tim said.

There was a gorse bush growing out of the side of the cliff. He had fallen right onto it. I held out a hand. Tim took it. I pulled him to safety and we both lay there in the sun, exhausted, glad to be alive.

We found the *Silver Medal* moored at the jetty and I steered it back towards the mainland. Eric was slumped on the deck. Johnny Nadler was down below, tied up with so much rope that only his head was showing. We weren't taking any chances after what had happened. We had already radioed ahead to the police. They would be waiting when we got to the mainland. Tim was standing next to me. We had left six dead bodies behind us on

Crocodile Island. Well, I warned you that it was going to be a horror story.

"I'm sorry I thought you were the killer," Tim said. He was looking even more sheepish than ... well, a sheep.

"It's all right, Tim," I said. "It's a mistake anyone could have made." He swayed on his feet and suddenly I felt sorry for him. "Do you want to sit down?" I asked. "It's going to take us a while to get back."

Tim shook his head. "No." He blushed. "I can't!"

"Why not?"

"That bush I fell into. It was very prickly. My bottom's full of..."

"What?"

"...needles!"

I pushed down on the throttle and the boat surged forward. Behind us, Crocodile Island shimmered in the morning mist until at last it had disappeared.